Miss Moo
Goes to the Beach

by Jeff Dinardo

illustrated by Dave Clegg

RED CHAIR PRESS

Miss Moo went to the beach.
She packed all the wrong things.

Her friend Henry came too.
He always packed the right things.

3

Henry took out the blanket,
an umbrella, and his book.

Miss Moo put on her skis, winter coat, and her warmest wooly hat.

After a short while Miss Moo
got very hot. "Time to go
swimming!" she said.

She grabbed her lawnmower and her
best dishes and ran to the water.
"Wait," said Henry running after her.
But he was too late.

"What a pretty fish," she gurgled.
"Would you like some tea?"

Henry pulled her out.
"You have to be careful!" he said.

"I'm bored," said Miss Moo.
"Let's play catch!"
She threw her ball to Henry.

"Goodness!" said Henry.
He got out of the way in time.

Miss Moo was hungry.
"I bought us some ice cream!" she said.

"Oh my!" said Henry.

"I had a fun day!" said Miss Moo.
"Thank you for coming with me."

"Tomorrow," she added,
"I think we should go skydiving!"
Henry sighed. "I think I'll stay home!"

Big Question: Do you think Miss Moo was thinking ahead when she packed for the beach?

Big Words:

gurgled: made with a bubbling sound

skydiving: the sport of jumping from an airplane

umbrella: used to protect one from sun or rain